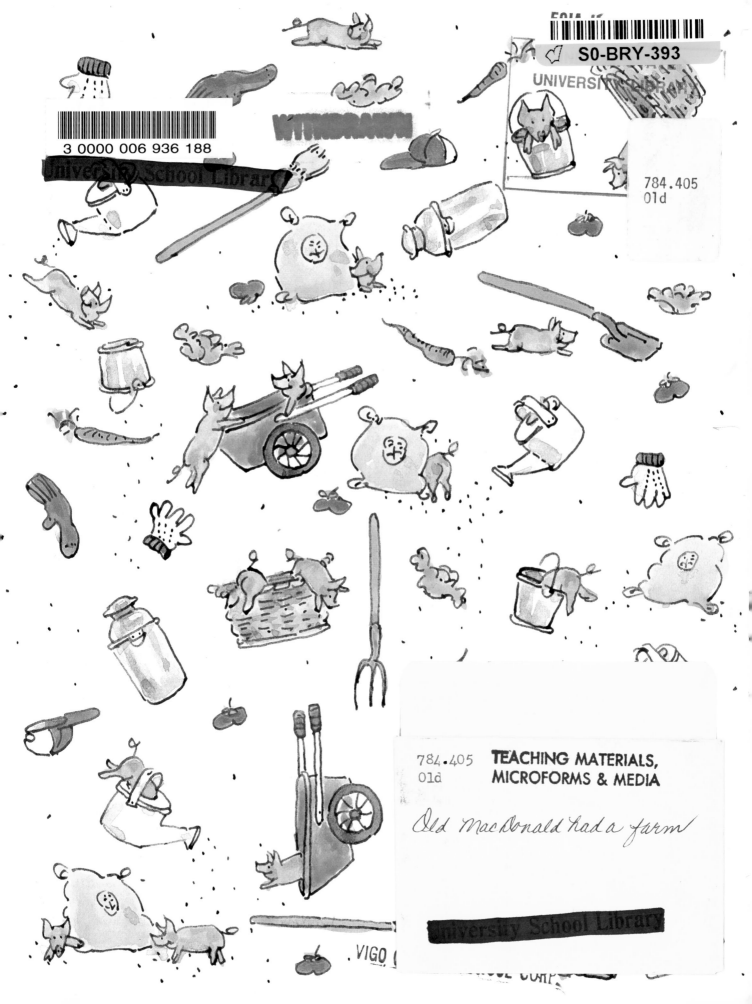

S0-BRY-393

3 0000 006 936 188

University School Library

784.405
Old

784.405
Old

TEACHING MATERIALS,
MICROFORMS & MEDIA

Old MacDonald had a farm

University School Library

Old MacDonald
Had a Farm

Tracey Campbell Pearson

Dial Books for Young Readers

E. P. Dutton, Inc. / NEW YORK

784.405
Old

For my Norwegian bachelor farmer

Published by Dial Books for Young Readers
A Division of E. P. Dutton, Inc.
2 Park Avenue
New York, New York 10016

Published simultaneously in Canada
by Fitzhenry & Whiteside Limited, Toronto

Copyright © 1984 by Tracey Campbell Pearson
All rights reserved
Design by Susan Lu

Library of Congress Cataloging in Publication Data
Old MacDonald had a farm.
Summary: The inhabitants of Old MacDonald's farm
are described, verse by verse.
1. Folk songs, American—Texts. [1. Folk songs, American.]
I. Pearson, Tracey Campbell, ill.
PZ8.3.0422 1984   784.4′05   83-18815
ISBN 0-8037-0068-7   ISBN 0-8037-0070-9 (lib. bdg.)

Printed in Hong Kong by South China Printing Co.
First Edition
(W)
10 9 8 7 6 5 4 3 2 1

The art for each picture consists of an ink, watercolor,
and gouache painting that is camera-separated
and reproduced in full color.

A Note About the Text
In keeping with the spirit of Old MacDonald Had a Farm,
*Tracey Campbell Pearson has added some of her own
verses to this folk song. Children are also encouraged
to make up their own words as they go along.*

Old MacDonald had a farm,
    e-i-e-i-o!
And on this farm he had a rooster,
    e-i-e-i-o!
With a cock-a-doodle here, and a cock-a-doodle there,
Here a cock, there a doodle, everywhere a cock-a-doodle.
Old MacDonald had a farm,
    e-i-e-i-o!

And on this farm he had a cat,
 e-i-e-i-o!
With a meow-meow here, and a meow-meow there,
Here a meow, there a meow, everywhere a meow-meow.
Here a cock, there a doodle, everywhere a cock-a-doodle.
Old MacDonald had a farm,
 e-i-e-i-o!

And on this farm he had a dog,
  e-i-e-i-o!
With a woof-woof here, and a woof-woof there,
Here a woof, there a woof, everywhere a woof-woof.
Here a meow, there a meow, everywhere a meow-meow.
Here a cock, there a doodle, everywhere a cock-a-doodle.
Old MacDonald had a farm,
  e-i-e-i-o!

And on this farm he had a wife,
  e-i-e-i-o!
With a gab-gab here, and a gab-gab there,
Here a gab, there a gab, everywhere a gab-gab.

Here a woof, there a woof, everywhere a woof-woof.
Here a meow, there a meow, everywhere a meow-meow.
Here a cock, there a doodle, everywhere a cock-a-doodle.
Old MacDonald had a farm,
    e-i-e-i-o!

And on this farm he had some geese,
  e-i-e-i-o!
With a honk-honk here, and a honk-honk there,
Here a honk, there a honk, everywhere a honk-honk.
Here a gab, there a gab, everywhere a gab-gab.
Here a woof, there a woof, everywhere a woof-woof.

Here a meow, there a meow, everywhere a meow-meow.
Here a cock, there a doodle, everywhere a cock-a-doodle.
Old MacDonald had a farm,
   e-i-e-i-o!

And on this farm he had some pigs,
  e-i-e-i-o!
With a grunt-grunt here, and a grunt-grunt there,
Here a grunt, there a grunt, everywhere a grunt-grunt.

Here a honk, there a honk, everywhere a honk-honk.
Here a gab, there a gab, everywhere a gab-gab.
Here a woof, there a woof, everywhere a woof-woof.
Here a meow, there a meow, everywhere a meow-meow.
Here a cock, there a doodle, everywhere a cock-a-doodle.
Old MacDonald had a farm,
    e-i-e-i-o!

University School Library

And on this farm he had some cows,
  e-i-e-i-o!
With a moo-moo here, and a moo-moo there,
Here a moo, there a moo, everywhere a moo-moo.
Here a grunt, there a grunt, everywhere a grunt-grunt.
Here a honk, there a honk, everywhere a honk-honk.

Here a gab, there a gab, everywhere a gab-gab.
Here a woof, there a woof, everywhere a woof-woof.
Here a meow, there a meow, everywhere a meow-meow.
Here a cock, there a doodle, everywhere a cock-a-doodle.
Old MacDonald had a farm,
   e-i-e-i-o!

And on this farm he had a mule,
   e-i-e-i-o!
With a hee-haw here, and a hee-haw there,
Here a hee, there a haw, everywhere a hee-haw.

Here a moo, there a moo, everywhere a moo-moo.
Here a grunt, there a grunt, everywhere a grunt-grunt.
Here a honk, there a honk, everywhere a honk-honk.
Here a gab, there a gab, everywhere a gab-gab.
Here a woof, there a woof, everywhere a woof-woof.
Here a meow, there a meow, everywhere a meow-meow.
Here a cock, there a doodle, everywhere a cock-a-doodle.
Old MacDonald had a farm,
   e-i-e-i-o!

And on this farm he had some sheep,
  e-i-e-i-o!
With a baa-baa here, and a baa-baa there,
Here a baa, there a baa, everywhere a baa-baa.
Here a hee, there a haw, everywhere a hee-haw.
Here a moo, there a moo, everywhere a moo-moo.
Here a grunt, there a grunt, everywhere a grunt-grunt.
Here a honk, there a honk, everywhere a honk-honk.
Here a gab, there a gab, everywhere a gab-gab.
Here a woof, there a woof, everywhere a woof-woof.
Here a meow, there a meow, everywhere a meow-meow.
Here a cock, there a doodle, everywhere a cock-a-doodle.
Old MacDonald had a farm,
  e-i-e-i-o!

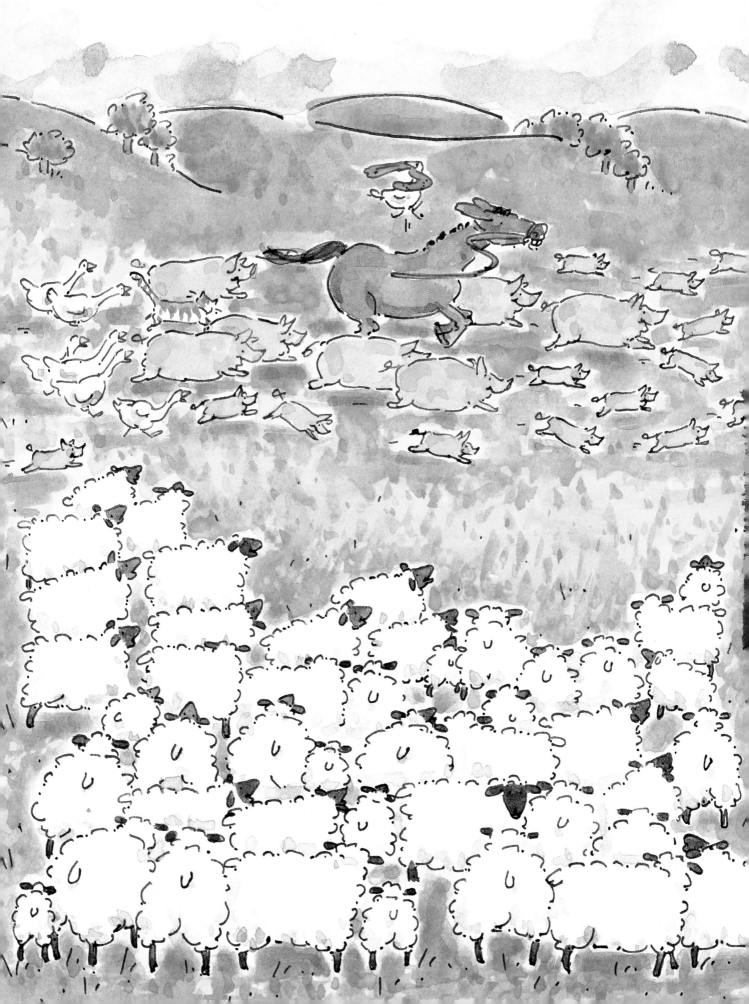

And on this farm he had a tractor,
  e-i-e-i-o!
With a putt-putt here, and a putt-putt there,
Here a putt, there a putt, everywhere a putt-putt.
Here a baa, there a baa, everywhere a baa-baa.
Here a hee, there a haw, everywhere a hee-haw.
Here a moo, there a moo, everywhere a moo-moo.
Here a grunt, there a grunt, everywhere a grunt-grunt.
Here a honk, there a honk, everywhere a honk-honk.

Here a gab, there a gab, everywhere a gab-gab.
Here a woof, there a woof, everywhere a woof-woof.
Here a meow, there a meow, everywhere a meow-meow.
Here a cock, there a doodle, everywhere a cock-a-doodle.
Old MacDonald had a farm,
   e-i-e-i-o!

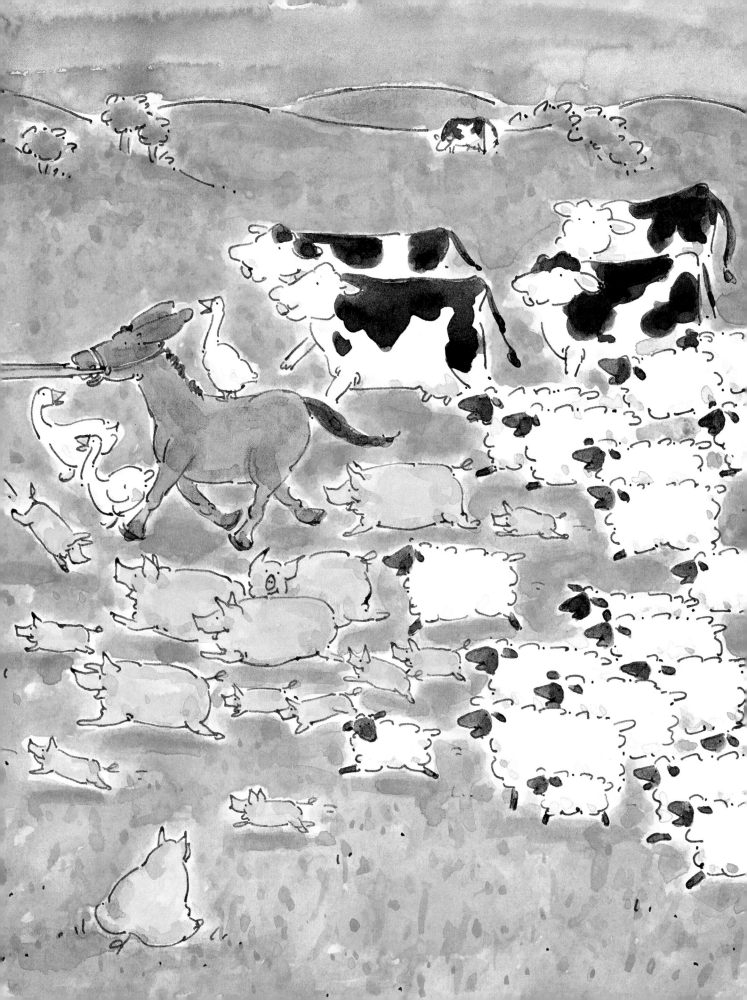

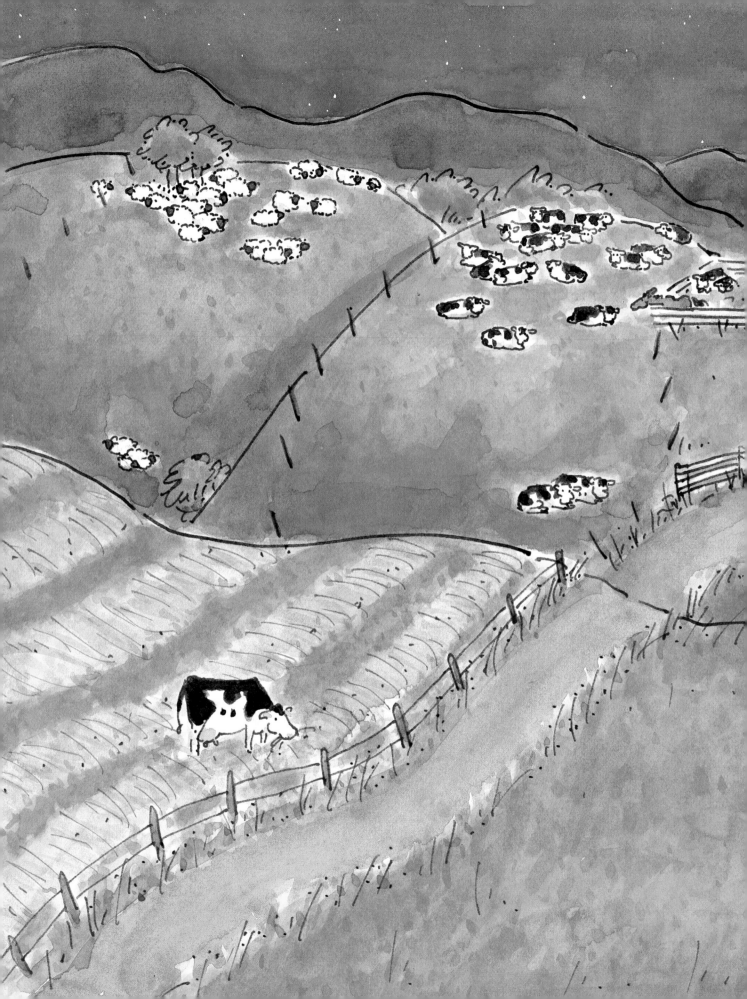

Old MacDonald had a farm,
     e-i-e-i-o!
He worked all day, then said goodnight,
     e-i-e-i-o!
With a snooze-snooze here, and a snooze-snooze there,
Here a snooze, there a snooze, everywhere a snooze-snooze.

Old MacDonald had a farm,
E-I-E-I-O!

Old MacDonald Had a Farm

2.
And on this farm he had a cat,
  e-i-e-i-o!
With a meow-meow here, and a meow-meow there,
Here a meow, there a meow, everywhere a meow-meow.
Here a cock, there a doodle, everywhere a cock-a-doodle.
Old MacDonald had a farm,
  e-i-e-i-o!

3.
And on this farm he had a dog,
  e-i-e-i-o!
With a woof-woof here, and a woof-woof there,
Here a woof, there a woof, everywhere a woof-woof.
Here a meow, there a meow, everywhere a meow-meow.
Here a cock, there a doodle, everywhere a cock-a-doodle.
Old MacDonald had a farm,
  e-i-e-i-o!
Etc....